Hanielle
The Christmas Fairy

K. R. Queen

Cover art by Angela M. Queen

ISBN: 9781672402927

This is a work of fiction. Names, characters, businesses, places, events and incidents are either the products of the author's imagination or used in a fictitious manner. Any resemblance to actual persons, living or dead, or actual events is purely coincidental.

To my boys,
hoping you will stay in love
with the magic and mystery
of Christmas
forever.

Chapter 1

Aislin "Ash" Fairchild had what began as a very bad Christmas Eve. On Christmas Eve she was returned to her group home (more properly called an "orphanage") after a few days in the emergency room.

Here is how it all began:

Ash lived with Edgud and Earlone Blackmun, the sort of people whom you might not believe even exist if you have never met the type. I say you might not believe they exist because they were as wicked (and therefore stupid) as two people can be. But they did exist, and Ash lived in their God-forsaken little house in the woods. Ash was placed with the Blackmuns when she was six years old, and she was now seven.

I so dearly wish you could have met precious Ash. Her black hair naturally formed loose ringlets that fell just to her shoulders. Her large, pleading, dark brown eyes were enough to turn anyone's heart to wax—anyone, that is, except the Blackmuns.

I suppose Edgud didn't mind Ash at first, but Earlone despised the little angel right from the start. Earlone was a severe woman, and she demanded that Ash do work on such a level that might be rightfully expected of a full-grown woman. The punishment inflicted on Ash for failure to keep up with Earlone's demands far exceeded the punishment that might be rightfully inflicted on anyone for such minor offenses, let alone a six-year-old girl! (And a very well-mannered six-year-old girl at that.)

But Earlone was not the worst part of Ash's stay with the Blackmuns. You see, Edgud sometimes went to church services at the local parish, and the church members were insistent that drinking even a single drop of alcohol was among the gravest sins in the whole world. As a result of the church's strong stance on strong drinks, Edgud was forced to keep his drinking to himself or risk being gossiped about!

As with many who drink in secret, Edgud's drinking was quite out of hand, and he became quite menacing when he drank. Ash was a clever little girl, and she could often escape Edgud's rage or other perversions before the situation became too dangerous for her. But she was not always so lucky.

On December 21st, sweet Ash was playing alone cheerfully in her toy-free room, and she was so fully immersed in the Christmas spirit—so fully immersed in letting her imagination fill her heart with joyous celebration—that she did not notice the familiar sound of Edgud's drunken babbling outside her door until it was too late. Edgud came crashing into Ash's room carrying Ash's purple dress, one of only three dresses she owned.

"Ya 'member asksking for a dress this murrnin," he slurred. "Well herrre ya go."

He threw the dress at her.

"Go ahead," he continued. "Put 'er awn."

"Mr. Blackmun," Ash said, adrenaline rushing into her stomach and pulsating into her chest and arms, "that's the dress my mommy bought me for my birthday."

"What kin'a lies are you tellin'? Just put it awn!"

"It's not Christmas yet."

"Dadgummit gurl, y'ask furr a dress so you can strut 'round pretendin' t' be pretty, and now you don't wawnt it?"

He took a stumbling lunge at her, but she jumped out of the way. He crashed headfirst into the bedpost, and when he rose his head was bleeding. Her eyes widened in horror as she realized the urgent danger of the situation. She made a dash for the door, but just as she reached the doorway, Earlone came around the corner.

"Wut in th'world is all that racket!" Earlone yelled, covering the doorway and stopping Ash from escaping. When Earlone saw Edgud cradling his head in his hands, with blood running through his fingers, Earlone screamed, "Y'lit'l demon! Wut in Jesus' name did you go an' do?"

Edgud pointed a bloody finger accusingly at Ash and said, "I wuz jus' tryna give her a presunt, an' she done got all feisty! She's a bad lit'l gurl, an' she needs a good wallopin', right thar on 'at bare behind. She need'a learn'a lesson!"

Edgud stumbled toward Ash and Earlone, fumblingly grabbed Ash by the hair, and began to drag her down the hallway. Ash screamed in pain and tried desperately to stand, but every time she got to her feet he yanked her head so hard that she fell back down and he could keep dragging her. Eventually she gave up and let her heels drag on the floor, whimpering in pain at everyone bump and turn.

Eventually, Edgud dropped (or, rather, threw) Ash onto the hardwood floor beside the living room sofa and stumbled into the kitchen to grab his favorite paddle—a massive, wooden monstrosity the local public school had used on middle school boys.

"Pull up yer skirt y'litt'l witch," Edgud said.

"Please don't—" Ash began, but Earlone cut her off.

"Y'heard him, y'litt'l monster!" Earlone said. "That'l be the last time you misbehave with my husbin'!"

Of course, Ash didn't know what Earlone even meant, she knew only that she desperately wanted to escape. Edgud always dealt her the most savage and bruising beatings when Earlone was around to witness it, and this seemed to make Earlone very happy.

Ash jumped to her feet and made another run for it. This time, she slipped past both of her oppressors, and before she knew it she was out the door of the trailer and running full speed into the pitch black forest.

"Dadgummit, get back herr raht naow!" Edgud bellowed out the front door of the trailer, but Ash had grown far more terrified of the Blackmuns than she was terrified of whatever wild dangers she might find in the nighttime forest. She plunged ahead.

Soon, the ominous light of the Blackmun's house had faded well out of sight, and she was alone with the sound of the gently rustling leaves, along with frogs, crickets, and coyotes. Her eyes adjusted to the dimly moonlit forest, and she could see her breath in the air. Frost glistened on the top layer of leaves at her feet. As her heart rate slowed to normal pace, Ash realized that it was terribly cold. She wore nothing more than her favorite green dress with red ribbons; thus, her legs and arms were fully exposed to the icy chill. And anyway, the thin material of the dress did very little to block the chill from the rest of her.

"Jesus, please help me," she said, looking up through the trees into the starry sky, littered with thin clouds. "Please help me."

Just then, she heard a howl, and within seconds she found herself surrounded by Edgud's prized hunting dogs. She made a run for the nearest tree, hoping to climb it high enough to be out of reach of the dogs, but one of the large and powerful dogs pounced on her and knocked her onto the icy, hard earth. She did not know it yet, but the reason the fall hurt so badly was that it broke her delicate little wrist.

Moments later, Edgud materialized out of the dark forest, holding a canned beer and smiling wickedly. He squeezed the can, smashing it, and threw it against a tree, which sent beer spraying out of it.

"What you think yer gonna do out herr, princ'ss? Ain't nowhere to go!"

Ash once again tried to run, but the dog bit her heel, piercing her stocking and drawing blood, and she once again sprawled to the ground, this time crying desperately.

"This'l teach'r t'run away," Edgud mumbled, grabbing a tree limb that was large enough to be more like a mace than the switch for which he intended to use it. He lifted the limb high over his drunken head, looking like some kind of pale, demonic ape, and brought it crashing down on innocent little Ash. The first couple of blows were horrifyingly painful. The third blow caught her in the head, and she was knocked unconscious.

Chapter 2

Ash woke up with blurry eyes and a fuzzy memory of what had happened. Everything around her was white, she could hear a chaotic chorus of machines beeping and people talking all around her, and a woman with soft, hazel eyes and wearing scrubs was standing over her.

"Hi sweetie," the woman said softly, brushing one of Ash's ringlets off of her cheek.

"Where am I?" Ash said.

"Your mommy and daddy brought you to the doctor. They're waiting just outside."

When the nurse spoke of "mommy and daddy," Ash remembered what had happened. She sat up very suddenly, startling the nurse. One nearby monitor attached by a wire to Ash began beeping loudly and rapidly.

"Shhh, it's ok sweetie. It's ok. Here, let's just lay dow—"

"Where are they? Please don't make me go back. Please don't let them hurt me again!"

Ash pulled her knees to her chest, wrapped her arms around her knees, buried her head into her arms, and began to sob uncontrollably.

The nurse gave Ash a reassuring rub on the shoulders, then left the room. A few minutes later, a different and less friendly woman came into Ash's room and began asking her questions about the Blackmuns. The questioning went on for quite some time, but eventually the woman left and the kind nurse returned and encouraged Ash to get some sleep. Ash's dreams were tormented by images of the Blackmun's (and past foster parents') abuses, and she woke in a panic several times throughout the night.

When the soft gold of morning had barely peeked into Ash's room, the caregiver from her old group home, Karen Tinkle, entered the room.

"Morning, Ash," Mrs. Tinkle said, putting her hands on her hips and scowling accusingly. "I guess I get to take you back now and try to find a way to bring in enough money to feed another mouth. You just can't help but cause trouble."

"I'm sorry," Ash said, feeling no desire to defend herself. Ash remembered Mrs. Tinkle all too well, and Mrs. Tinkle became furious when any child was bold enough to correct her assumptions, no matter how little evidence there was for them. The moment Mrs. Tinkle declared an assumption true or false, that assumption became gospel in the group home—and woe to the poor child who rejected that gospel.

"Well, come on then!" Mrs. Tinkle said, waving her arms with such animation that her massive puff of blonde-highlighted hair shifted back and forth on her head like a loose helmet.

"Yes ma'am," Ash said, sliding off of the plain, white mattress and dragging herself weakly to Mrs. Tinkle.

Ash had a cast on one wrist, a large bandage wrapped tightly around her ribs, and another bandage wrapped around her head. She felt as if every last inch of bone and muscle in her entire body were made of hot cement, and she found it very difficult to take even a single step.

"Where are Mr. and Mrs. Blackmun?" Ash asked.

"They're in trouble because of you. If you would just do what you're told instead of being so rebellious, this wouldn't happen." Mrs. Tinkle had beckoned to Ash's bruises as she said it.

"I'm sorry," Ash said again.

On the way out, Ash's nurse from the night before smiled sadly at her and said, "Merry Christmas, sweetie."

"Yeah," Ash said defeatedly, keeping her eyes glued to the floor. "Merry Christmas."

A few steps outside the hospital, Ash looked up at Mrs. Tinkle and asked, "Is it Christmas today?"

"No," Mrs. Tinkle snapped. "It's Christmas Eve. And don't even think about asking for presents. There is no way Santa will bring you anything tonight—you are definitely on the naughty list."

Ash crinkled her sore little brow and nodded, then looked back down at the pavement as her eyes began to fill with tears. In the end, she let only a single tear fall, but she shed many more tears in her heart where no one could see.

Upon return to the group home, Mrs. Tinkle put Ash right to work. When Ash struggled to move as fast as Mrs. Tinkle wanted, Mrs. Tinkle growled that Ash's injuries weren't that bad and that she deserved it anyway.

"You're just the worthless pile of ash I sent to the Blackmuns," Mrs. Tinkle said. "Step to it, you little rat."

Ash winced in pain multiple times, and she was physically incapable of staying ahead of Mrs. Tinkle's demands. By the time the sun went down, but long before bedtime, Mrs. Tinkle was completely fed up with Ash's "belligerent" slowness.

"You know what?" Mrs. Tinkle said. "Just get out. Go to your room—or are you too stupid to remember where it is?"

"No ma'am," Ash said, dropping her lukewarm dishrag into the sink. "I know where it is. I'm sorry."

Ash was relieved to be done with her work, and she was incredibly relieved to once more sleep in a room where she would be free from the fear of Edgud that had tormented her every night for the past year. All the children in the group home knew that if they resisted Mrs. Tinkle for very long, she would eventually give up and stick them in front of a television or send them to their rooms so that she could go do whatever laziness she was in the mood for that day. The place was boring, Mrs. Tinkle was perpetually rude, and the children were shamefully neglected. But anything was better than life with the Blackmuns.

When Ash made her way down the hallway, a cool wind of tranquility washed over her, seeming to rush up from within her. She took a long, deep breath and felt the exhale wash the anxiety out of her sweet heart. She paused at a window in the hallway that cast a soft orange glow from the streetlights onto the carpet below. She looked out the window at the young moon and emerging stars over the desolate streets, waiting for every last ripple of turmoil within her to relax into total stillness.

Ash folded her hands as well as she could with the cast on her wrist, kept her eyes fixed on the sky, and said, "Thank you, Jesus."

Chapter 3

Ash walked into her dark, empty bedroom and sat down on the edge of the stiff bed, which was practically the only thing in the room besides the rickety, wooden nightstand beside it. But just as she started laying her bruised and weary body down to sleep, something in the corner of the room caught her attention.

Standing in the farthest corner of the room from Ash was a little figurine of a person, about 6 inches tall, dressed in intensely white robes, and adorned with some of the most beautiful wings Ash had ever seen—wings that made the most radiant butterfly wings look like they were drawn with a crayon.

"Hello there," Ash said to the figurine, supposing it to be a toy. "I wonder who left you here."

"No one left me here," the figurine responded.

Ash gasped. It was not that some-*thing* was in her room—this was some-*one*!

"Don't be afraid," the miniature person said. "I have been sent to spend Christmas with you. We will have lots of fun."

"Who are you?"

"Wouldn't it first be better to ask *what* I am?"

"What are you?"

"A fairy, of course! Haven't you been a good girl and been reading your fairy tales? Never mind, I know that you have. Would you like to spend Christmas with me?"

"Mrs. Tinkle doesn't want me to leave at night. She says only bad things happen at night."

"Mrs. Tinkle has no idea what 'bad' means. I am older and smarter than Mrs. Tinkle. You can listen to me, even if Mrs. Tinkle tells you not to."

"But isn't it dangerous to go outside at night? Everyone says that—not just Mrs. Tinkle."

"I can protect you from anything."

"But you're so small. What if a big, scary man tries to hurt us?"

"Dear child, my size has nothing to do whether I can protect you. And I can promise you that tonight you will see things much more dangerous than a big, scary man if you come with me."

Ash frowned and said, "Then I don't want to go!"

"You don't think I can protect you? You think I am lying to you?"

"Umm... I guess not. But I will get in big trouble, and Mrs. Tinkle will make me scrub the toilets with a toothbrush again! She is already very mad at me for being so bad."

"My child, you are not bad. You are as good as a person can be on this side of death. You must not listen to the Accuser."

"I don't understand."

"Ah yes, my Lord did warn me not to say what you are not ready to hear. You are a child, too full of wisdom to have any need for knowledge." The fairy fluttered her beautiful wings and flitted from the corner of the room to the nightstand beside Ash. When the moon beams reflected off her wings, they sparkled with rich, heavenly colors that have rarely been seen in this world, and that are impossible to describe to anyone who has not seen them. The fairy held out her hand to Ash and said, "Come along! I *pinky promise* that you will not get in any trouble. I will make Mrs. Tinkle sleep until we get back."

Ash exclaimed, "You can do that?"

The fairy waved her hands in a wide arc, as if she were spinning a large (well, large for her) wheel. A bluish, green mist formed between her hands, and began swirling like a miniature hurricane. Then she pushed her hands toward the door, and the mist crawled off the nightstand, across the floor, and out the door.

"There," the fairy said. "That will do it."

"What was that?"

"What was the mist?"

"Yes."

"It was sleep."

"You know how to make sleep?"

"I can make probably anything you can imagine."

"Even a doll house?"

The fairy smiled warmly and said, "We are going to have so much fun together."

"Where are we going?" Ash asked.

"First, we will visit someone I know you really want to meet."

"Who?"

"You'll have more fun if it's a surprise. But don't worry! It won't take us long to get there."

The fairy once more held out her hand, inviting Ash to take it.

"What is your name?"

"Hanielle is the nearest word I can give you to my name. Really it is best not to ask my name. It is too wonderful. You may think of me as the Christmas Fairy."

"What do you mean?"

"If you know a person's real name, then you really know that person—my name is older than your whole world and is impossible for your kind to handle all at once."

"I don't understand."

"I'm sorry. You would think I would be better at this after all these thousands of years talking to your kind. Anyway, are you coming?"

Hanielle flitted from the nightstand to the bed, landing right beside Ash. The very sight of her filled Ash with great beams of happiness, as if her entire spirit were suddenly made of flowers and blue skies.

"Okay."

"Now, here's what I can tell you. We will be taking a journey along the path of Christmas. Very few have been allowed to see what you will see. This journey will be awful, but it will be wonderful!"

"What do you mean by 'the path of Christmas'? I thought Christmas was just a day."

"Christmas is far more than just a day, and it has been traveling along the Earth for many many years. You are going to go see bits and pieces of the great Christmas journey!"

"Why?"

"Because you have never seen it before."

"It sounds like it will take a long time and be very boring."

"Sweet child, you must not worry. You will be younger when the journey is done than you were when it began."

"I don't want to be younger."

"Oh, but you do. I can see it quite plainly in the deepest corners of your heart."

"Do you have any candy?"

"I don't. But the man I'm taking you to see has more candy than anyone in the whole world."

"Okay, then let's go."

Hanielle smiled again and held out her hand one last time, fluttering her wings as if warming up for the coming flight. Ash finally gave in and put her pointer finger into Hanielle's tiny hand. Although Hanielle's hand was little more than the eraser end of a pencil, touching it was like touching electricity— only instead of pain, it shocked Ash with pleasure. Hanielle lifted her other hand straight into the air, then sharply dropped it. The room around Ash began to twist into all sorts of unnatural shapes. It was like the walls and floor were made of water and were being blown around by powerful winds. Then, as quickly as the turmoil began, it ended.

Ash found that as far as she could see in every direction, she was surrounded by snow and ice.

Chapter 4

"We're supposed to meet someone out here?" Ash said to Hanielle, who was flying beside her head.

"That's right! He lives just past that iceberg."

"I'm cold."

Indeed, Ash did not realize just how dangerously cold it was. It was so cold that she could have caught frostbite within mere seconds. After all, they were standing in the North Pole!

"Oh dear, I should know better than to bring you into the North Pole without dressing you a little better."

Hanielle stretched out her arms and pointed open hands toward Ash, holding them very still. Little white sparks soon began to fly out of Hanielle's hands. Suddenly, Ash felt a rush of warmth, and when she looked down she was dressed in a massive coat and boots. The coat covered her entire body and seemed to be made of something both heavier and yet softer than any throw blanket she had ever touched. It was delightful.

"The North Pole!" Ash exclaimed. "You're taking me to see Santa!"

"Oh no! I have spoiled the surprise!"

"I'm sorry."

"Don't be sorry! Anyone in your shoes with half an ounce of sense would be thrilled to be where you are right now."

Just then, a most terrifying thing happened. From around a nearby iceberg came a humongous, snow-white monster, at least 10 feet tall. It had the build of a chimpanzee; huge, pointed teeth; and angry, red eyes. It spotted Ash and began walking towards her and Hanielle, knuckles dragging on the ground and leaving a trail in the snow.

"Hanielle?" Ash said, quivering with terror. "What do we do?"

At the sound of Ash's voice, the monster grunted deeper and louder than any bear or tiger, and it began to run, galloping sideways on all fours. Soon it was moving toward them at a terrific speed. Its mouth had begun to froth and foam, streaming disgusting globs of saliva into the air around its mouth.

"The abominable snowman!" Hanielle declared. "You don't run across her every day!"

"It's gonna eat me!"

Hanielle fluttered between Ash and the charging monster, wings sparkling in the cold sunlight, and she began to swing her arms up in wide arcs like she was attempting to summon something from below the ground. She swung her arms in the same motion several times before anything magical began to happen, and by that time the abominable snowman was far too close for comfort. Ash fell to the fetal position, buried her head into her knees, and shut her eyes as tightly as possible.

Nothing happened. All the commotion of the monster's running had stopped, and there was nothing but silence, broken only slightly by the icy wind and the sound of snow peppering the sides of the icebergs.

Ash ventured a peek to see what was happening. The abominable snowman stood motionless no more than a few yards away, grinning at her like some great childish ogre. Hanielle sat square on its nose, kicking her feet like someone sitting on a lakeside dock.

"What did you do?" Ash said, rising to her feet.

"You can't tell? I knocked the abominable-ness out of her. Now she's about as harmful as a giant puppy, which I suppose still isn't perfectly harmless, but at least she doesn't want to eat you anymore! It's much easier to knock the badness out of an animal than out of one of your kind. Humans have become very good at holding on tightly to abominations."

"What is an abomination?"

"Oh, it's just a really bad thing. But enough of such talk. We have a schedule to keep!"

"Is it safe?" Ash said, staring nervously at the abominable snowman. "It won't get hungry again and come after us?"

"It's a little safe. Would you like to touch her? People don't get to touch abominable snowmen very often!"

"I don't know," Ash said, very reluctant to come any closer to the monster.

"Don't worry! I promised you that nothing could hurt you and I will not break my promise. Come on, give her foot a little rub."

Hanielle fluttered into a standing position on the beast's nose and beckoned Ash to come nearer.

"Uh, okay."

Ash timidly approached the abominable snowman and placed a shaky hand on its foot. She was surprised at how soft its fur was, though it was still not nearly as soft as the coat Hanielle had made for her. The abominable snowman looked down at her with a massive, dumb smile plastered across its face. Even with the badness knocked out of it, the abominable snowman still looked rather abominable to Ash. She was barely as tall as its knees, even though its legs were very short compared to the rest of its body. Just remembering the slobbering beast charging at her only a few moments ago made her shudder.

"Ok, I'm ready to go," Ash said brusquely.

Hanielle laughed and said, "Onward then!"

The pair trekked across the barren tundra, but presently the barrenness gave way to all sorts of new sights and sounds. They came upon a well-marked path, decorated on either side by red and green ribbons, twinkling multicolored lights, and gilded metal rails. The lights blinked to the tune of familiar Christmas music, and a colorful array of decorations stretched ahead for as far as the eye could see. The sight of it took Ash's breath away.

Shortly after they entered the decorated area, they came upon an incredibly large snowman on the right side of the path. In his mouth was a corn cob pipe, and he had a button nose and two eyes made out of coal, and he wore an old silk top hat. But then the eyes seemed to blink. Ash paused to concentrate on the snowman's face, but she took several stumbling steps back and fell into a sitting position when the snowman leaned down face-to-face with her, and said, "Merry Christmas! What are you doing here?"

"Hanielle?" Ash said, wondering if she should be worried.

"I brought her," Hanielle said to the snowman.

"Hanielle!" the snowman exclaimed. "How wonderful to see you again. Come to see the old man?"

"If he's not too busy for little Ash."

"Oh no, he would always make time for little Ash."

"He knows me?" Ash said.

"Of course he knows you! He knows all the little boys and girls."

"Mrs. Tinkle told me I was on the naughty list."

At that, the snowman burst into the loudest explosion of laughter that Ash had ever heard. It seemed to echo off of every iceberg within a ten mile radius. His head was thrown back, and his entire massive body heaved with the voluminous peals of laughter.

When he finished laughing, the snowman leaned back forward and said, "We haven't been formally introduced." He held out his scrawny, tree-branch hand, and said, "I'm Frosty. Frosty the Snowman."

"Frosty!" Ash exclaimed. "You're so big!"

"Sweet Ash, you have not spent one second of your life on the naughty list. Mrs. Tinkle, on the other hand"—and Frosty leaned down and smiled—"she has been on the naughty list her whole life."

Ash laughed out loud for joy and relief, threw her arms around Frosty, and said, "Thank you, Frosty! Thank you!" But she quickly pulled back, shivering—snowmen are much too cold to hug for long.

Frosty once more leaned down to Ash, and this time he said, "You are quite welcome. Now…Catch me if you can!" And with that, he sped off like a train. It was incredible how fast Frosty was. Ash wondered how he could move like that without any legs. There was no visible sign of something driving Frosty forward; instead it looked like he was just sort of floating or gliding along the ground, kicking up huge splashes of snow on both sides.

"We'd better keep up!" Hanielle said. "You have to follow Frosty if you want to see Santa!"

"Oh no!" Ash said. "He's so fast!"

"We can do it. Come on!"

Hanielle sped ahead of Ash, helping her stay on track when she would have otherwise lost sight of Frosty. They wove all throughout what must surely have been Christmasville, for it was the most thoroughly Christmas decorated town there could ever be. Candy canes hung from every tree; strings of Christmas lights adorned the fences, houses, and occasionally even adorned the jolly, portly people wandering around the place. The people seemed not to notice the great Frosty chase, or, if they did, the chase seemed altogether typical to them, because they never paused for long before going back to their decorating, gardening, or whatever other busy work they were up to. They seemed neither happy nor grumpy; they simply went about their business.

Unfortunately, Ash began to grow tired. She had not been gaining any ground on Frosty during the chase, and now she was falling behind. She did not notice the tiny reindeer that had escaped from the nearby house until it was too late, and although she tried to jump aside last second to avoid the collision, her foot caught on the deer, and the two sprawled in the snow. Frosty would certainly be long gone now.

"No!" Ash cried. "How will I see Santa if I don't catch Frosty?"

"I didn't say you had to *catch* Frosty," Hanielle laughed. "Only that you had to *follow* him. Well, you followed him, and now you've arrived!"

Just then, Ash noticed that the reindeer she had collided with had jumped into the air, but several seconds later it had not yet landed back on the ground—rather, the little reindeer remained suspended in the air, looking down its bright red nose at Ash with some mix of curiosity and indignance at having been bowled over.

"Rudolph's little girl," Hanielle said, pointing to the levitating reindeer. "She's a sassy little one, isn't she? But, then, so are you—it's one of your best qualities!"

"You mean Rudolph the red-nosed reindeer?" Ash exclaimed.

"Of course! What other Rudolph would be just outside Santa's house?"

Ash's eyes widened. Could she really be standing outside Santa's house? Hanielle pointed to the majestic, two-story house the reindeer had come from. Sure enough, the green and red sign hanging from the large, mostly glass door had these words printed on it in elegant, sweeping cursive: "Mr. and Mrs. Clause."

Chapter 5

"Can I ring the doorbell?" Ash asked.

"Of course you can! Mrs. Clause always comes to the door with the most warm and delicious cookies."

Ash beamed at Hanielle and would have hugged her had it been possible to hug such a small creature, then eagerly approached the large door and rang the doorbell. No sooner had Ash's finger touched the bell than a kindly old woman opened the door, smiling directly at Ash.

"Merry Christmas," the woman said. "Would you like a cookie?"

The woman was indeed holding a plate of steaming chocolate chip cookies.

"Yes, please," Ash said.

"Come in, come in. Santa has been looking forward to meeting you."

Ash glanced back at Hanielle, who was flying at eye level just behind her, checking to make sure it was okay to follow Mrs. Clause. Hanielle flicked her wrists in a shooing motion and whispered, "Go with her!"

Mrs. Clause was slow getting around, and she walked with absolutely no sense of urgency. Ash followed closely behind her, munching on the very best cookie she had ever had—the perfect balance of warmth and gooey-ness. The cookie disappeared very quickly into Ash's happy little tummy, although, unknown to her, a little glob of chocolate remained on the edge of her mouth and cheek.

The house was even more incredible on the inside than on the outside. Presents, wrapped and unwrapped, were *everywhere*. The presents were mostly children's toys, but there were other items as well: microwaves, coffee mugs, watches, socks—so many socks!—etc. The house was basically a mansion converted into a massive Christmas warehouse.

Perhaps the most striking thing about the house was the pointy-eared workers busily attending to the gifts. Ash, of course, knew these workers to be elves, and there were hundreds of them! They wore green clothes with red buttons, and they formed dozens of little teams, each diligently working on either building or wrapping or packing a gift.

Mrs. Clause led Ash and Hanielle across the expansive warehouse to a door at the back of the room. She knocked lightly on the door.

A booming voice emerged from the other side of the door: "Come in!"

Mrs. Clause opened the door, and held it open for Ash to enter. Sitting just inside, at a desk that was covered in letters and was well-lit by a lamp and by the most thoroughly decorated Christmas tree there has ever been, was a very large man dressed in candy-apple-red clothes and a hat of the same color, all with white fur cuffs. It was Santa Clause!

"Ash," Santa said warmly with his jolly, deep voice—a big smile pushing out his plump, blushed cheeks, "How wonderful it is to see you!"

"Santa!" Ash said, running up to him and hugging his leg. "Mrs. Tinkle told me I was on the naughty list, and I was so sad. I'm not on the naughty list, am I? I'm sorry I got Mr. and Mrs. Blackmun in trouble."

"Ho ho ho!" Santa bellowed. "Ash, my dear, you have been on the nice list your whole life. You are a very good girl. That's why you're here."

"But if I've always been on the good list, then why haven't you always brought me presents? Last year I didn't get anything. Mrs. Blackmun said it was because I was so naughty."

Santa looked sympathetically down at Ash and said, "There are some houses I am not allowed to go into. The Blackmuns will not let me into their house, and there is nothing I can do about it."

"But I would have let you in!" Ash cried. "You could have brought something to just me. They didn't have to know!"

"Have a seat right here on my lap," Santa said, deflecting the difficult conversation. Ash happily climbed into his lap, and Santa said, "Now tell me: what would you like for Christmas?"

"Can I have a family that loves me and doesn't hurt me?"

Santa furrowed his bushy, white eyebrows and looked thoughtfully at the floor for a long while. Finally, he said, "I'm afraid I don't have that."

"What do you mean? I thought you have everything and can do anything!"

"I do! Well, I have everything that can be made by my incredibly talented elves. They can make any-*thing* you want—just not any-*one*. They can make any kind of toy you can think of."

"Oh Santa, I do want a dollhouse, but I *really* want a family who doesn't hate me and hurt me."

"But maybe a dollhouse would make you feel better?"

Ash's eyes fell, and she said, "No, thank you."

Although she retained her kind demeanor, Ash was obviously disappointed by Santa being powerless to help her in the way she really needed it. All he knew how to do was give people trinkets, and even then he was limited if the adults would not let him into their houses. Who would mend Ash's broken heart?

Santa looked rather dejected, and he sat there for several seconds in silence with little Ash on his knee. All that could be heard was the faint sound of the elves outside, bustling around and talking rapidly amongst themselves in a mad rush to finish their toils. After all, it was Christmas Eve!

Finally, Santa mumbled, "I wish you could meet my father. He could help you."

Hanielle flitted up from behind Ash, approached within a couple inches of Santa's face, and said, "Why can't she meet your father?"

Santa's eyes lit up, and he said, "By my sleigh, you're right!"

Santa removed his thin, metal glasses; rose from his well-padded chair; and made his way out of his office, motioning for the others to follow. The very second Santa emerged from his office, every single elf in the entire house went completely still and silent, all eyes fixed on him.

Ash looked questioningly at Santa, and he beamed down at her and winked. Then he looked up at all the silent elves who seemed to be waiting for something.

Santa took a deep breath, and bellowed, "Ho ho ho!" so loudly that it rattled Ash's teeth and made her ears ring for many minutes afterwards.

At once, the elves resumed their work, now with renewed fervor. Some of them got so carried away and got to moving so quickly that they became impossible to see with the naked eye, except for the occasional green and red blur.

Santa led Ash and Hanielle down to the side of the room. At the far wall was a staircase that spiraled up to the second story of the mansion. The stairs were made of dark wood—perhaps cherry wood—and the rail going up the stairs was covered in a spiral garland, sprinkled with white Christmas lights and little multicolored bows. At the top of the stairs was a small, wooden door that was so small and modest that it looked almost out of place in Santa's mansion.

"Is this an attic?" Ash asked. "I used to live in an attic."

"It is my father's room," Santa said, reaching for the door handle. "It is a great hall, like the days of old. (My father is *very* old.) But I must warn you: it might just be the merriest place in the whole world!"

Chapter 6

Ash did not know what Santa meant by "a great hall," but it sounded to her like a perfectly fun place. Santa opened the door, and an incredible sight greeted Ash's eyes. They entered a huge, long, rectangular room, somewhat like a chapel, with two massive tables right down the middle of it, covered with every sort of food and drink imaginable. In between the tables was a long fireplace in which roared the largest fire Ash had ever seen—the tallest licks of the raging flame must have been at least as tall as a house! The mighty fire roared, crackled, and popped with such force that Ash was almost afraid of it. The ceiling rose to incredible heights (in fact, it was *impossibly* high for what Ash had seen from the outside), and long windows were cut into the sides of the stone walls, casting diagonal bars of sunlight down onto the tables below. Flaming torches lined the walls on both sides. Massive men with massive beards wearing massive fur coats lined the tables, heartily stuffing their faces with food and drink.

"Those men are making a very big mess in your house," Ash said, looking up at Santa with deep concern.

"Ho ho ho!" Santa bellowed. "They're always like this on Christmas Eve! Follow me."

Sitting on what looked like a throne at the far end of the hall was the most massive of all the men. He had a long, white beard, and he wore a red hooded robe with white fur cuffs, which looked like really nothing more than an older version of Santa's outfit, only in a darker shade of red. If all the other men in the hall were happy, this man was absolutely ecstatic! His merriment seemed to be erupting within him in mighty storms of laughter and revelry.

As Santa approached the throne, followed closely by Ash and Hanielle, the man in the throne threw his hands in the air, slinging his oversized mug around, and splashing quite a lot of his frothy, brownish-orange drink onto the floor. The jolly man said, "Cheers to another wonderful Christmas, my boy! Welcome, treasured guests, to Christmas Hall! Eat, drink, and be merry, for Christmas shall be over soon!"

Honestly, the intensity of the joyous feast in the hall made Ash more uneasy than happy, but she trusted Santa, and if not Santa, then she very deeply trusted Hanielle, for surely no one untrustworthy could have brought her this far.

"This," Santa said, turning to Ash and pointing to the man on the throne, "is Father Christmas—*my* father. Sadly, I cannot stay with you, for there is much to do! Ho ho ho, and merry Christmas!"

Santa turned abruptly and sped out of Christmas Hall, and Ash felt sure that he was leaving just as much because of discomfort as he was leaving due to any need to keep a schedule.

"Santa is a good kid," Father Christmas said. "He just doesn't know how to give the *really* difficult gifts. But he'll learn. Cheers!"

When Father Christmas yelled "cheers," everyone in the hall erupted into an even louder chorus of shouting, eating, and drinking. Wooden mugs crashed violently into each other, sending their drinks splashing toward the sky; food and drink flew all over the place; and many of them threw their heads back in uproarious laughter. A handful of them fell backwards out of their chairs, and most of them got back up. The rest lay on the floor snoring, with the foam from their frothy drinks dripping from their beards onto the rough, wood floor.

"What gifts?" Ash said. She was standing just below the throne and looking up at the jolly monster of a man.

"Why, *happiness*, of course!" Father Christmas roared. "Isn't that what you're here for? Of course it is! Happiness is what *everyone* is looking for! Cheers!"

"I've never heard of you Mr. Christmas. You're Santa's daddy?"

"I certainly am! Santa has worked hard to follow in my footsteps and make everyone happy, but he thinks the best way to make you happy is with toys—what nonsense! The only people who can be happy with such trinkets are the spoiled children whose parents can buy the toys and the spoiled business owners who make them! Happiness doesn't come from toys, my dear, it comes from in here." He was pointing vigorously at his own heart.

"Do you give people presents, Mr. Christmas?"

"What greater present is there than happiness?" Father Christmas shouted. "Cheers!" (Each time Father Christmas shouted "cheers," the hall erupted once more into manic celebration.)

"Could you have made me happy while I was with the Blackmuns?"

Father Christmas fell silent and furrowed his brow just as Santa Clause had done, and the family resemblance between Santa Clause and Father Christmas was then quite obvious to Ash. This was the first time Father Christmas's demeanor had displayed anything other than unbridled joy. He threw a boulder-like fist up and leaned his cheek heavily on it, seeming to think with all his might.

Finally, Father Christmas spoke again, this time with a more serious tone: "Dear girl, you must take every opportunity that you can to be happy. *Truly* happy. You get only one life to live, and you don't want to waste it being sad all the time!"

"How could I be happy when Mr. Blackmun was hurting me every day, and calling me mean names? Or when my mommy hates me and doesn't want to see me? Can you help me be happy?"

Ash's eyes were welling up with tears, and she fixed her large, dark, pleading eyes right on Father Christmas, silently begging him to help. Again, Father Christmas seemed thoroughly stumped. The celebration in the great hall had begun to die down, because by now a majority of the men had fallen asleep on the floor, some of them piled on top of each other. The few who remained awake were clearly in such a stupor that they no longer had the life in them to celebrate with the amount of energy they had before.

Father Christmas sounded very grave indeed when, after an even longer pause, he practically whispered, "It is the *enemy*. He wants you to be sad. You must not give in!"

The way Father Christmas said "enemy" sent a terrible shiver down Ash's spine, and she said, "The enemy?"

"Yes! He would steal your happiness, but you must cling to it."

"How do I be happy when everyone is hurting me?"

Father Christmas's shoulders slumped, and his face fell into a state of almost total depression, a mightier depression than Ash had ever seen.

"I wish you could meet my father," Father Christmas said defeatedly, after the longest pause of all. "He could help you."

Hanielle flew up to Father Christmas and said, "Would you like me to take sweet Ash to see your father?"

"My father does not live here," Father Christmas said.

"I know exactly where your father lives," Hanielle replied rather pointedly.

"If you are one who can take her to see my father, then I could not stop you even if I wanted to. You may be on your merry way—indeed, you must! Cheers!"

Only one man was left awake. He was sitting with his back leaned against the wall, slumped down until his chin touched his chest, and he held up his mug and slurred out weakly in response to Father Christmas, "sschairz." Then he cracked his mug for a toast against the forehead of a nearby man who had been long asleep, guzzled what was left in his mug (though most of it actually poured out of the sides of his mouth and onto his neck and shoulders), dropped his mug to the floor, and fell asleep where he sat. Ash giggled.

By now, the golden sunlight streaming through the sky-high windows had been replaced by dark blue and purple twilight and faint moonbeams. The hall was perhaps even more majestic now, as the cold twilight colors mixed with the fiery glow within the hall to produce a grand, glowing tranquility. But there was something not quite right about it—that is, besides the slobbering men on the floor.

"It's so pretty!" Ash exclaimed.

But Father Christmas did not respond, for he had fallen asleep right there on his throne.

Chapter 7

Faint sadness washed over Ash. But in that glorious great hall it was difficult to be *too* sad—instead, sadness simply lurked below the surface. In the great hall of Father Christmas, it was easy to sweep sadness under the rug and temporarily suppress it. Temporarily.

"Are you ready to go?" Hanielle asked.

"I don't know," Ash replied. "What if we stay until they wake up?"

"They will not wake up for a very long time," Hanielle said. "I'm afraid you would get frightfully bored and frightfully sad if you tried to stay here for that long."

"Okay," Ash said, looking curiously up at Father Christmas. What a titan of a man! He looked so strong, and kind, and joyful. Ash began to wonder if she loved Father Christmas even more than she loved Santa Clause! She decided she loved them both very much, even if they could not help her.

Ash turned away from Father Christmas and towards the table, and said, "What's that?" She was pointing at a small plate of some dessert-looking food that seemed to be the only untouched plate on the whole table.

"They're scones," Hanielle said. "Do you want one?"

"Yes, please," Ash said.

"Help yourself!"

Ash glanced back at Father Christmas, then tiptoed over to the table, careful not to step on any of the arms, legs, or snoring heads in her path. She climbed up onto the table, trying to avoid getting any of the messy food, drink, or slobber on the beautiful coat Hanielle had made for her. She grabbed just one scone and climbed back down. It was filled with strawberry jam, and when she took a bite, it was positively bursting with rich, sugary, fruity flavors.

Ash smiled quite happily at Hanielle, and said, "Thank you! This is wonderful!"

Hanielle smiled back and said, "Every food in Christmas Hall is wonderful. Are you ready now?"

"Yes."

"Then let's be off!"

Hanielle flew in a wide arc, then sped toward the door from which they had entered Christmas Hall. Ash had to run rather quickly to keep up with Hanielle, and she was out of breath by the time they reached the door at the others side of the great hall. Fortunately, Hanielle paused in the doorway, which, you will remember, was also at the top of the spiral staircase. Hanielle took a slower pace going down the stairs.

"We mustn't run on the stairs," Hanielle said. "We can't have you breaking any bones on Christmas Eve!"

For the first time that night, Ash realized that she was no longer wearing her cast or bandages, but that her wrist, head, and ribs felt just fine—better than ever, in fact!

"You fixed me!" Ash exclaimed.

"I'm sorry to say that I did not. You will still have to heal when we return."

"Is this a dream?"

"Not in the way you think of dreaming."

"I don't understand."

Hanielle did not respond, so Ash chose to remain silent with her as they continued down the stairs. All the commotion that had been churning in Santa's warehouse earlier had completely stopped, and all the lights were now off. The large room was very barely lit by the Christmas lights strung along the walls. Throughout Santa's house, not a creature was stirring, not even a mouse.

"Where is everyone?" Ash asked.

"Come outside, and you will see!"

Hanielle led Ash through the eerie, silent mansion and out the front door. The sun was fully set by now, and stars twinkled brightly in the sky, seeming to almost dance with excitement. The moon was larger than Ash had ever seen it. It seemed that every single citizen of Christmasville, all bundled in large coats and scarves, was standing outside and looking up at the sky.

"What's going on?" Ash said.

"Shh," Hanielle said, putting her tiny finger up to her mouth, then using the same finger to point up at the sky. Just then, there was a loud scrambling and scraping noise from behind Ash, just over her head. She let out a little scream and ducked.

"Hurry!" Hanielle said. "Look!"

Ash opened her eyes, lifted her face to the sky, and gasped. Flying at what Ash just knew must be the speed of light was a sleigh, pulled through the starry night sky by eight reindeer. Santa sat in the sleigh, looking larger than life. A monstrously large sack, overflowing with presents, sat right behind him in the sleigh. Before Ash knew it, the sleigh had sped out of sight, off to leave toys with all the good little boys and girls.

The citizens of Christmasville burst into a chorus of cheers and Christmas carols. They danced, and sang, and hugged, and high-fived one another. A group of young children and a few elves could be seen ice skating with impressive precision, jumping and twirling on the ice. The little girls on the ice wore sparkling dresses that reminded Ash somewhat of Hanielle's wings. The town was ablaze with Christmas lights, shimmering and shining on every house and tree in sight. Frosty was running around with a broomstick, followed by a trail of laughing children. Mothers and fathers held each other tightly and kissed under the mistletoe. The baby reindeer Ash had run into earlier approached from behind and nuzzled her hand, looking up into her eyes with a loving, if slightly timid, expression. Its nose was shining as brightly as any light in sight. Ash smiled at the little deer and patted its head. The reindeer did a somersault in midair, just for Ash, then pranced off to join in the merriment.

"I love it," Ash said softly, feeling the magic of the moment sparkle in her heart.

"It's time to go see Father Christmas's father," Hanielle said. "But if we are going to go see him, we must leave this magical place and go to an even more magical place."

"What place is more magical than this?" Ash said.

"History!" Hanielle said.

"History?"

"Yes! Nothing you have seen tonight has been or will ever be recorded in the history books, because it is a myth."

"Myth!" Ash exclaimed. "You mean it's not real?"

"I didn't say it's not real. Myths are colorful paintings where the paint is the realest things the painter knows. Myths are nothing more than the piling up of a thousand realities into one place. What you have seen tonight is, in some ways, more real than the world you live in. But the best is yet to come! Sometimes, myths like this actually break into history, and that is where we are going next. We're going to where Father Christmas cannot go—to meet *his* father."

"Who is Father Christmas's father?"

"You must see for yourself! Are you ready?"

"I guess so…" Ash was dearly enjoying the joyous celebration of Christmasville, and she very much did not want to leave. But she trusted Hanielle, and she was therefore willing to follow.

Hanielle flitted down to Ash's hand, wrapped around Ash's wrist in a bear hug, and flapped her radiant wings with such force that she and Ash were lifted off the ground. Ash let out a delighted scream as Christmasville grew smaller and smaller below her the higher they rose.

Upon seeing Ash fly into the air, the crowd below cheered their loudest cheer of all. And then, like a snap, the crowd was gone.

Chapter 8

Rather than fly farther up into the sky, Hanielle's flight seemed to carry Ash more *up* than it is usually possible to fly. Instead of flying *up* into the sky, they flew *up* into a new world. It seemed as if they had busted out of the ground of this new world without moving a single pebble; or perhaps as if the world around them were made of wind and mist, but then suddenly solidified.

It was nighttime. Ash found herself standing a stone's throw away from a large, marble building with stately pillars at the front entrance, lit by a handful of torches. Just past the building rose a grassy hill, with a series of stone buildings built onto the side of it, and the grass was sprinkled occasionally with boulders. The streets and buildings at the bottom of the hill and around Ash were all made of stone. She felt she was surrounded by the ruins of some little ancient town, except the buildings were not run down at all. Rather, they were in perfectly good condition and seemed to be fairly new.

Ash stood beside a lonely alleyway, and a putrid, disgusting stench was emerging from it. She looked down the alley and spotted an unnaturally skinny man dressed in thin, brown cloth. He was sitting on the ground. His feet were small and horribly deformed, and he was more covered in dust and muck than any pig you have ever seen. It was terribly cold, and the man was shivering violently.

Ash looked questioningly at Hanielle, but Hanielle was fixated on the man, and tiny tears had formed a series of crystals on her cheeks. The man saw Ash and began to crawl toward her. It was immediately clear to Ash that his legs did not work, for they dragged behind him as uselessly as a fish tail.

Ash became frightened, and she was about to run from the groveling creature of a man, but Hanielle said, "Don't be afraid. Wait. Watch. Listen."

Reluctantly, Ash stopped and waited, even as the beggar crawled to within five feet of her.

"Unclean!" The beggar suddenly shouted, causing Ash to give a start and causing her heart to spring into action.

Ash glanced back at Hanielle, hoping to be released this time from the prohibition on running away, but Hanielle said nothing and did nothing— rather, she remained tearfully fixated on the beggar. Ash knew she could not bring herself to let the beggar touch her, and she was about to run when a nearby voice arrested the beggar's movements and made Ash jump again, although not quite as violently this time.

The voice had calmly said, "In the name of Jesus, I greet you."

Ash turned to locate source of the voice. A man with a white beard much like Santa's and Father Christmas's beards, and dressed in humble robes, was approaching the beggar from the direction of the pillared building. He and the beggar were the only two people in sight.

"Unclean!" The man shouted again, this time at the approaching man. But the man continued approaching, eventually walking right up to the beggar.

"Good evening," the man said warmly to the beggar.

"Do you have a coin or a few crumbs of bread for me?" the beggar said.

"I do," the man replied, and handed the beggar a cloth pouch full of coins that jingled like Santa's sleigh, and a steaming loaf of bread, and a little wooden cup of steaming hot tea. "Eat, drink, and be satisfied."

Then the generous man took off his outer robe, wrapped it around the beggar, and spoke again: "Be warm. And may the Lord Jesus bless you tenfold."

"Thank you!" the beggar cried, with an enormous smile on his face. "Praise be to the Lord Jesus!"

"Do you believe in Him?" the generous man asked.

"I do believe in Him, for you are a great man," the beggar replied.

"I am nothing. He is everything. And if you believe in Him, I command you to rise to your feet."

"I have not been able to walk since I was born!"

"If the Lord is willing, you shall dance in the streets this very night. Rise and be healed!"

The beggar looked up at the generous man with total wonderment on his face. He hesitantly gathered his legs under him, and tested one leg first, then the other. Quite suddenly, he sprang into the air and began prancing and jumping around, shouting with all his might.

"I can walk!" the beggar shouted. "I am brand new!"

Then the beggar knelt to the ground and began to cry tears of joy.

The generous man said, "Go and tell everyone that it is by the power of Jesus that you now walk, and do not dare to speak of me to anyone, or else you will lose your legs as quickly as you received them."

"Bless you!" the beggar said, and threw his arms around the generous man, then ran off into the night, jumping and dancing in the streets.

Hanielle flew to Ash and landed on her shoulder, pointed at the generous man, and said, "That is Father Christmas's father! He goes by many names: Nicholas of Myra, Nicholas the Wonderworker, or you might know him best as *Saint Nicholas*."

"Saint Nicholas!" Ash whispered. "I thought Santa was Saint Nicholas."

"As you can see, Saint Nicholas is a close relative of Santa's. As you can see, they are so very different."

Saint Nicholas approached Ash and said, "In the name of Jesus, I greet you."

"Hello," Ash said cheerfully. "That was so nice of you!"

"The Lord has been much kinder to me than I could be to anyone."

"Why didn't you let him tell anyone about you?"

"Gifts given in secret are nearest to the heart of the Lord."

"Father Christmas said you could help me be happy."

"Father Christmas? I know of Christmas, but not *Father* Christmas."

"He said you were his father."

"I may be. I am afraid I have no happiness to give to you. Only in my father will you find happiness, and more!"

"Oh no…" Ash said, feeling the crushing sadness rush back into her heart. Tears began to run gently down her cheeks, and she said, "Every time I ask someone to help me, they cannot help. They just send me to someone else."

Saint Nicholas knelt down to the ground, put his hand under Ash's chin and lifted her face, and said, "What makes you sad, my child?"

"No one will love me. My mommy is mad at me because I am ugly, and she wishes I was never born. The Blackmuns hurted me every day, and Mrs. Tinkle says I am nasty and stupid and bad."

Ash fell to her knees and began to sob. Saint Nicholas, still on his knees, grabbed her and pulled her up so that he could hug her. Ash wrapped her arms tightly around his neck and sobbed bitterly into his shoulder. Saint Nicholas cried with her for some time. Eventually, he pulled her back, put his hands on her shoulders, smiled through his tears, and said, "I *promise* with all of my heart that it will not always be like this. I *promise*."

46

"But I want someone to love me right now!" Ash cried, and buried her face back into Saint Nicholas's shoulder.

"My father will love you," Saint Nicholas whispered. "You must meet my father." Then he looked up at Hanielle, who was floating just overhead, and said, "Hanielle, will you take her to see my father?"

"I will," Hanielle said solemnly.

Saint Nicholas looked back at Ash, brushed the ringlets off of her tear-stained face, and said, "My father created Christmas. He will help you."

"Everyone has said that their father can help me, but no one can," Ash said faintly, feeling the weight of the sorrow and cynicism pressing in on her spirit, threatening to drown it.

"I *promise* you will not be disappointed again," Saint Nicholas said. "My father is the one you have been looking for."

"Is there really an *enemy* trying to steal my happiness from me?"

Saint Nicholas's face became very grave, and he said, "Yes. But my father is greater than the enemy."

When Father Christmas had spoken of the enemy, it had terrified Ash and given her a deep, numinous chill that threatened to send her spirit into a frenzy of fear and dread. But when Saint Nicholas spoke of the enemy, Ash simply felt anger—an emotion she did not feel very often—and it was the enemy she found that was angry with. When Father Christmas spoke of the enemy, he seemed to speak of a terrible dragon that could be fought, but never beaten, like it was only a matter of time before all hope was lost. When Saint Nicholas spoke of the enemy, he seemed to speak of a malignant parasite that was certainly dangerous, but for which it was only a matter of time before it was successfully removed and no longer allowed to hurt anyone. Ash was now very mad at the enemy, and she wanted to go give him a piece of her mind.

"Where is the enemy?" Ash said, feeling brave.

"He is around," Saint Nicholas said. "But, sweet child, you should never go looking for him. No, you must go find my father."

Ash looked to Hanielle as if to ask if Saint Nicholas was right, and Hanielle nodded.

"Okay," Ash said. "Hanielle says she can take me."

"May the Lord Jesus bless you and keep you," Saint Nicholas said. He humbly bowed, then walked back the way he had come, soon veering to the right and disappearing behind one of the ancient stone buildings.

"Where will we go now?" Ash said.

"There is only one more place to go," Hanielle said. "But you must stay close to me. It is very dangerous."

Chapter 9

Ash shuddered at Hanielle's ominous words, and she said, "Do we have to go there?"

"You are there every day," Hanielle said. "I am merely taking you with new eyes."

"I don't understand."

"We have travelled nearly the full history of Christmas," Hanielle said. "But we haven't travelled to the history of *this* Christmas."

"What?"

"Oh dear, I am afraid I can say no more to help you understand. We simply must go. Will you trust me?"

"Yes."

Although Ash did not understand what Hanielle was saying, and although she was afraid of where they were going, she trusted Hanielle so completely that she was willing to follow her anywhere. Hanielle fluttered down to Ash's hand, grabbed it, and began to fly in wide circles around her, causing Ash to spin. Soon, they were spinning faster than any person could spin without help from a fairy, and the world around Ash became a blur. Then, all light around her, which was already very minor, melted completely away.

Hanielle stopped spinning, and Ash found herself standing in total darkness, so that the only thing she could see was Hanielle, who glowed with familiar sparkling radiance, even in the dark, though it seemed she did not cast any light outside of herself with which to see anything else.

"It's so dark," Ash said, nervously. "I'm scared."

Hanielle flutter very close to Ash's face, and said, "You must be very careful *not* to be afraid."

"But I can't see!"

"Your eyes are adjusting."

"I will be able to see soon?"

"You will. You've just never been here in the way that you're here now."

"Where are we?"

"A few blocks away from Mrs. Tinkle's house, right beside the store."

Ash knew just the store Hanielle was talking about, and she hated that store. When Ash was only four years old, Mrs. Tinkle began making her walk to the store every week with a list of groceries, and Ash had to walk back carrying them all. It was worse because she walked right by the house of one of the wealthiest men in the entire city, and his beautiful wife, beautiful children, and beautiful house had always filled Ash with deep longing for a better life. The grand house taunted Ash every week as she walked by.

And just past the wealthy man's house was the church he attended when he wasn't too busy. It was a towering, majestic building of the finest architecture. Each week, Ash wearily lugged groceries past that grand chapel and wondered how they had so much money for stained glass windows, elegant spires, and even a bunch of golden plates for people to pile their money into, but did not have enough money to give even the most meager food, clothes, or toys to the impoverished children at her group home. Maybe she and her fellow orphans were too ugly or dirty.

Ash said, "I don't see the store anywhere."

"Wait for a moment," Hanielle responded. "You will soon have eyes to see."

Dim shades of gray had begun to emerge from the darkness, and they steadily began forming blurry (but increasingly solid) shapes, most of them in motion. More and more, the shadows and gray images took on solid shapes and increasingly dazzling colors. More and more, Ash felt she had very good cause to be afraid. The shapes that emerged from the darkness were creatures! And the creatures were either too wonderful or too horrid to look at for long without falling into total worship or into psychotic terror. The incredible creatures were crashing into one another with great explosions of light, and—stranger—great gushes of darkness, like rivers of shadow. Ash's ears were apparently also adjusting, because as the images solidified around her, so did the sounds the creatures were making: great rumbling growls that would have sent the abominable snowman fleeing in terror, shouts that sounded like sunshine itself, and great crashes that reverberated through the place with the force of two planets smashing into one other. Ash was witnessing a cosmic battle right before her eyes!

"What is this?" Ash said with a quivering voice.

"It is, as I said, the history of *this* Christmas," Hanielle replied. "Just over there, past those demons, you are finishing up your dishes earlier today."

"Demons!"

"You didn't know that's what you were seeing? This is the real world. It is to your world what your world is to the myths. You have never seen anything as real as this, which is why it took you so long to see or hear anything."

While Hanielle was still speaking, one of the demons took notice of her and Ash. It bared its terrible teeth, cackled like a hyena, and began running (or flying—it was difficult to tell) toward them. Hanielle sprang between Ash and the charging demon, her body burst into bold flashes of what looked like precious jewels, and she quite suddenly grew to at least the size of a gorilla. A giant broadsword made entirely of something like fire appeared in her hand. She gripped the sword with both hands and took a flying swing at the demon. The sword struck the demon, and it screeched like metal caught under the wheels of a train. Sharp beams of light pierced the air and stung Ash. When the stinging light had subsided, the demon was gone.

Hanielle immediately shrank back down to her normal size—or had she just revealed her normal size?—and flitted back to Ash.

"What was that?" Ash said.

"That was fear," Hanielle said. "He is one of the enemy's deadliest weapons."

Ash gasped and said, "Is the enemy *here*?"

"You will see him soon."

"I thought you were taking me to see Saint Nicholas's father!" Ash cried.

"I certainly am."

"If you can be so big, why do you stay so small?"

"Your heart is still beating very fast, and I took my full form for only a brief moment. Your kind is not used to seeing angels in real form, so we must take whatever form will not distract you from what we're trying to tell you. If I had introduced my *full* self to you tonight, and remained that big, you wouldn't have listened to me! You would have been too scared."

"You're an angel!"

Hanielle smiled and said, "You may call me what you like. I will happily remain your Christmas fairy, if that's what you want. Now, let's go! We don't want to miss the big event, but we first have to make the journey."

Hanielle flew ahead, and Ash followed as well as she could. One could not simply walk around there; it required great concentration to navigate, or even just to follow Hanielle. It would be impossible to describe to you the glories and horrors of that heavenly place. Ash's eyes sometimes grew dim, and at other times everything around her became exceedingly vivid; so vivid, in fact, that she would wonder if she had ever seen anything at all before then—as if every past memory were actually just a dream, and she had just woken up for the first time. Some areas were glorious: paved with something like gold, lined with buildings adorned with pearls and diamonds, and flowing with rivers of glass. Other areas were terrible: seeming to be made of fire, and waste, and darkness.

As they went on their way, they came upon one whom Ash recognized to be a man. He looked familiar, but she was not sure why. He was curled up in the fetal position in one of the horrid fiery areas, and he seemed to be in a great deal of pain. In his mouth was a large pacifier, just like a baby's pacifier, and he was sucking on it with extreme effort. He was so shockingly thin that he looked like nothing more than skin stretched thinly over a skeleton. He looked as if he had not eaten in many years. Lying around him were a woman and two small children, all sucking on similar pacifiers, and all in agony.

"We have to help them!" Ash cried.

"We have tried to feed them," Hanielle said. "But they won't take the pacifiers out of their mouths."

"You can't take them out yourself?"

"By now, taking it out would destroy him." She was pointing at the terribly skinny man. "I don't know about the others. You may not have realized it, but you know this man! He is the wealthy man who lives beside the church. Those pacifiers are his wealth. The woman and children are his family. There is nothing in your world that starves the spirit faster than wealth."

Ash's eyes widened. No wonder she had recognized the man. He was her neighbor!

"What can we do?" Ash cried. "They are so sick!"

"I don't know if there is anything left to do," Hanielle replied, with sorrow heavy in her voice.

"The enemy gave him that pacifier long ago, and it has ruined him and his family. We must continue on."

No sooner than the wealthy man was out of sight, they came upon a small group of disgusting, hideous people. They had a greenish color to them, and some substance of the same green color was oozing and dripping off of their skin (or perhaps their skin itself was dripping), and they each carried with them weapons of various sizes. The hideous people were completely surrounded by demons, which had formed a barrier around them. Angels hovered around the demon barrier and launched attacks on it, but the barrier remained firm. It seemed the angels were trying to get to the people.

"Why do those angels want to hurt those people?" Ash said.

"No, sweet child, not *hurt* them. The angels are trying to *rescue* them. The demons are feeding them poison, and they die a little bit more very day. But the demons have also given them weapons to fight off the angels with, and so the people have gotten very good at fighting angels. Even when the angels break through the barrier, these people will not let themselves be rescued. See?"

One angel had broken through the barrier of demons and had snatched up the most disgusting of the green people, but the person being rescued began to frantically strike the angel with his club. Meanwhile, the other green people began attacking both the angel and the person the angel was trying to rescue. Soon, one of the demons grabbed the person and yanked him back out of the angel's grasp. The barrier rapidly formed once more to block the angel out.

"But why would he fight the angel like that!" Ash exclaimed.

"He knows nothing of angels and demons, for he sees only with his animal eyes and not his spiritual eyes. You know him as well—he is the pastor at the church beside the wealthy man's house! He has become truly spectacular at fighting the angels who would rescue him. The others with him are members of the church. But look!"

Ash turned back to the church in time to see a woman of astounding beauty approaching the barrier of demons. Her face shone with the radiance of a star, and she held weapons in her hands that also seemed to be made of starlight. She easily passed by the demon barrier—as if they were not allowed to touch her—and she offered her weapons to the green people. Some of them attacked her, though their attacks were comically futile, while others dropped their old weapons and accepted her new weapons. Those with the new weapons instantly looked a little healthier and less green than the others. Those who accepted the glorious woman's weapons followed her out of the demon barrier and out of sight.

"What happened?" Ash said.

"It's Christmas Eve!" Hanielle said. "The woman showed them the power of faith and kindness, and those who accepted it were rescued. You may not remember her, but when you were very young she often brought you gifts and prayed over you when no one else would. She is a mighty warrior of light and a friend of the angels. She is also a member of that church."

"She isn't an angel?"

"That's right! You could go see her tomorrow if you wanted. In fact, you should. She is very kind to children."

"Oh, I hope I get to see her. Will I know her when I see her?"

"Of course, sweet child. Once you have seen a person as they really are, you cannot un-see them. Now, we must be going. It is almost time!"

Chapter 10

Hanielle sped ahead with some urgency, occasionally springing into her true size and glory to fight off demons, but always immediately shrinking back down when the demons had been dealt with. The longer they traveled, the more frequent the attacks became, and every attack was aimed at Ash. But Hanielle was able to keep her promise that Ash would remain safe, and every last drop of fear within Ash eventually disappeared, even as Hanielle mightily fended off the most horrible creatures there could ever be.

Ash knew when they had arrived, because she saw something that she could never have predicted. Standing just ahead, and looking towards the sky was a radiantly beautiful little girl whom she immediately recognized as herself!

"It's me!" Ash exclaimed. "I am so pretty!"

"No mirror could show you how beautiful you really are, sweet child, but you are so very beautiful. Remember what I told you? Where we are right now, you have just finished your chores and you are now standing at the window—do you remember?"

"I remember."

"What happened at the window?"

"Nothing happened."

"Are you sure?"

Demons began converging on Ash's past self, but a team of angels formed a barrier around her, much like the demon barrier around the church. Just behind Ash's past self, a demon was devouring a woman whom Ash recognized as Mrs. Tinkle, and Mrs. Tinkle was crying out in an agony deeper than death. The other children in her group home remained well-guarded by the angels, though the demons often got through long enough to scratch the poor children, leaving terrible gashes.

The battle had risen in volume—or Ash was hearing it more clearly—and the intensity of the scene threatened to overwhelm Ash and send her into a panic. And then Ash saw the one Father Christmas and Saint Nicholas had warned her so fervently about. She saw *the enemy*. It was a colossal, snarling beast, with spikes down its spine, razor teeth and claws, and a vortex of swirling darkness at its center, as if its heart and very life were nothing more than a black hole that threatened to suck everyone and everything in its path into a lonely, burning darkness. The enemy saw the glorious spirit of Ash standing in the window and he hated her because she was so much more beautiful than him. He roared thunderously, and the sky and air all around them broke into something like a fiery lightning storm. Then he charged at Ash's past self with raging ferocity.

"Help me!" Ash shrieked, seeing the grave danger her past self was in. "Help!"

Just as she cried out for help, the terrible beast stopped in its tracks. Light suddenly came pouring into the night. The light filled every corner of the place and every corner of Ash's being. The light was so pure that she could feel it flowing inside her like a fresh spring wind and cleansing her from the inside. With the light came a booming sound like the sound of a thousand tornadoes, or a thousand trumpets, or a thousand years of laughter. This grand, fearful noise would have typically shattered Ash's (or anyone's) eardrums, but here it only filled her with life. The sky above and earth below became filled with the most vivid colors of blue, green, and gold, as well as a white so pure that she realized she had never seen *real* white before, only a dirty attempt at whiteness. Springing out of the sky, the ground, and even the air were blossoms of colors the human eye has never seen and melodies the human ear has never heard. Great gushing streams of water emerged from the ground, and the water was sweet and refreshing even to touch. Everything the light reached sprang to life, and the light reached everything.

The demons, and the enemy most of all, looked to the sky with horror on their faces, for the life in the light had struck a fatal blow to the enemy and his demons. The angels looked to the sky with such pure adoration as to make a mother looking upon her newborn or a groom seeing his bride walk down the aisle look apathetic. Ash followed their gazes and looked to the sky. Descending to the earth was nothing more than a small basket, but it was obvious that the great springs of life that were filling up the place were flowing down from the basket.

The basket landed on the ground in front of Ash, and a great hush fell upon the entire place—a stillness so complete that the drop of a feather would have seemed a terrible commotion. Ash looked down into the basket and saw only a baby. How could such life come from a baby?

Ash looked up at Hanielle, and said, "What's happening?"

"It is Christmas," Hanielle replied. "A gift for you."

Just then, the spirit of Ash's past self said, in a voice that echoed with the golden radiance of springtime, "Thank you, Jesus."

Ash remember her tranquility from earlier that night, and how she had thanked Jesus for the peace within her that had far surpassed what made sense. Ash then understood that the grand battle had been raging around her all night, even though she could not see it, and that this baby had descended to the earth and silenced the battle for her.

Ash looked down at the baby, and she loved him. She picked up the baby, held him in her arms, and kissed him.

Ash looked back up at Hanielle and said, "Why did everyone stop fighting when this baby got here?"

"Every Christmas Eve, when the moon is young, there is a moment of profound stillness within those who have the ears to hear it. In every heart that listens, all anxiety, anger, and sadness fade away, and all that remains are peace, joy, and love. That moment is a gift. This baby is Jesus, whom the demons fear and whom the angels adore. He is the One Saint Nicholas calls 'Father.' There never would have been Christmas without this baby, because this baby is the very Creator of Christmas and the very best gift that has ever been given! This baby is what happened when the Father of all fathers gave everything he had—even his own self!—as a gift."

"This baby is the one who can help me?"

"When the baby in your arms was born, He was like a comet of heaven crashing into the earth, and He brought with Him all of the things that would be your very favorite things if you only knew to want them. Indeed, look around you! One thing He brought with him was *hope*, for when He grew up He showed you a glimpse of what the world will one day be like. Even now, the seeds of heaven planted by Him have begun to grow into thriving gardens all over the Earth. Because of Him, you stumble upon little pockets of heaven every day. But one day you will get all of it!"

"I will get all of *heaven*?"

"That's right! Heaven will blossom upon the entire surface of the Earth! To look at that baby and be thankful for the peace and hope He brought with Him; to long for more and more of heaven to come to Earth; to get to work planting and watering little gardens of heaven wherever you are; to love with all your heart that baby and everything he became—*that* is the great hope and joy of Christmas. It is the great hope and joy of life!"

Ash looked once more down at baby Jesus, and she loved Him more than anything or anyone she had ever loved. She longed with pangs stronger than the deepest hunger to spend the rest of her life with Him.

"He is with you everywhere you go," Hanielle said. "When you lay gifts at the feet of poor, sad, helpless people, you are laying those gifts at the feet of Jesus. Even when you can't see Him, He is with you and He is in you. Your families may have the power to keep out Santa, but *no one* has the power to keep out Jesus. In some ways, you already knew He was with you—that's why you cried out to Him in your greatest need, and that's why you thanked Him for your incredible peace. And because you already had a sliver of the truth within you, He has let you see so much more of it. And how wonderful it is to know that the best is yet to come! You are so beautiful and so fortunate, sweet Ash. You have come face-to-face with the One who makes beauty from ashes."

Chapter 11

The heavenly world melted away, and Ash was now standing with empty arms on the very familiar doorstep of Mrs. Tinkle's group home.

Hanielle said, "It is time for us to say goodbye."

Ash did not respond, because she was very sad. She looked pleadingly at Hanielle.

Hanielle continued: "My child, I have been your fairy for many years—longer than you have been alive! I have never left your side."

"But I don't want you to go where I can't see you! Can I stay with you?"

"Sweet Ash, you must not be sad and you must not be afraid. In a few hours, it will be Christmas Day! It is a time for celebration! And I promise that just as I have been with you during your entire life up to now, I will be with you forever."

Ash began to cry tears of sorrow and of joy. She smiled through the tears and said, "Thank you, Hanielle. I will never forget you."

"Run along, now! The sleep spell on Mrs. Tinkle is about to wear off, and you don't want her to find you out here!"

Without waiting for Ash to reply, Hanielle fluttered in a figure eight, then threw out her hands and began spiraling and splashing colors all over the place, like a punctured balloon made of liquid jewels. Then, with one final sparkle of her dazzling wings, Hanielle vanished.

Ash ran into her group home and tiptoed down the hallway, past Mrs. Tinkle's room, and into her humble little bedroom. Sitting on Ash's bed was the most amazing dollhouse she had ever seen! A letter lay beside the dollhouse. Ash ran to the letter and opened it, and the letter read as follows:

Dear Ash,

Santa was very upset that he could not bring this lovely dollhouse to you himself. He asked me to drop it off here. He said his elves made the prettiest dollhouse in the whole world, just for you!

May you have a truly joyful Christmas!

Sincerely,
Hanielle

Ash jumped up and down, giddy with happiness. Then, she remembered the sickly wealthy man down the street, and the beautiful woman at the church, and the wondrous generosity of Saint Nicholas, and the Father of Saint Nicholas giving her the precious baby in the basket, and she got an idea that she knew Santa wouldn't mind. She took the amazing dollhouse off her bed and set it on the floor, then crawled into bed. Her wrist, ribs, and head were terribly sore again. But she did not notice the pain because she was too excited trying to think of someone she could give her new dollhouse to the next morning, the morning of Christmas!

Beautiful Ash looked out her window at the twinkling stars, took a deep and peaceful breath, and whispered, "Thank you, Jesus." Then, she rolled over and fell into a most delightful sleep, for she was overflowing with Christmas spirit.

Thank you

Thank you for reading *Hanielle: The Christmas Fairy*!

If you enjoyed *Hanielle*, there are a couple of simple ways you can help it get noticed and reach more readers:
   (1) Write a review on Amazon
   (2) Share it with your friends

And, of course, I will be very thankful for any and all feedback, whether it be positive or constructive.

Made in the USA
Las Vegas, NV
16 December 2022